ΣX LIBRIS

THIS BOOK BELONGS TO:

VOLUME ONE

GREEK MYTHS

JACQUELINE MORLEY

Published in Great Britain in MMXVII by
Scribblers, an imprint of
The Salariya Book Company Ltd
25 Marlborough Place,
Brighton BN1 1UB
www.salariya.com

HB ISBN-13: 978-1-910706-81-7

3 5 7 9 8 6 4 2

A CIP catalogue record for this book is available
from the British Library.

Printed and bound in China.

Reprinted in MMXVIII

Illustrations by:

Patrick Brooks
Persephone
King Midas

Oscar Galvan
The Story of Arachne
Meleager and the Blazing Log

Ivana G Kuman
Echo and Narcissus
Atalanta and the Golden Apples

Alida Massari
Prometheus and Pandora
Eros and Psyche

Visit
www.salariya.com
for our online catalogue and
free fun stuff.

GREEK MYTHS

JACQUELINE MORLEY

Illustrations by:
Patrick Brooks
Oscar Galvan
Ivana G Kuman
Alida Massari

VOLUME ONE

SCRIBBLERS
a SALARIYA *imprint*

CONTENTS

INTRODUCTION

Here is a collection of stories that have all the ingredients for a good read:

Monsters, giants, fire-breathing serpents, brave heroes, wicked sorceresses, winged sandals, helmets of invisibility, all the stuff of fairy tales but with something else besides.

Fairy tales belong to a make-believe world where good characters end up happy and wicked stepmothers are punished. The stories in this book

are myths, and with myths you can't be certain this will happen. This is what makes them so gripping. When Theseus slays a monster and returns rejoicing to his father, you can't be sure there'll be a happy homecoming. When Laocoon fights with deadly sea serpents you can't assume he'll win. Myths are the world's oldest stories. All peoples have them. They are our earliest attempts to make sense of the world. Long before science came along to account for most things, people evolved stories that answered the big questions of life: who made the earth and the sun and put the stars in the sky, how did we get here? Where do we go when we die?

More than any others, the myths of the ancient Greeks have kept their hold on people's imagination through the centuries. They are great stories with unforgettable happenings – a feast for young readers and young listeners alike.

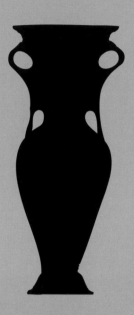

PROMETHEUS AND PANDORA

This is how the Ancient Greeks imagined the world began. In the beginning, they said, Mother Earth created the world we live in. She made the land, the mountains, the rivers and the seas. Then she married the starry sky and gave birth to the living creatures: the lion, the horse, the eagle, and all the birds and beasts we know today. But there were no rules then about what was good or bad, and some of the creatures she made were horrible monsters, giants with a hundred arms or one eye in their forehead, and lawless beings like the Titans, a race of gods who were the first

9

rulers of the world. Their king, Cronos, was so horrible that his son Zeus overthrew him. This was a happy thing for everyone for Zeus was much more reasonable than his father and kept the wild Titans in order. He imprisoned Cronos in chains and forced Atlas, the brawniest Titan of them all, to hold the great weight of the sky on his shoulders for ever.

Zeus and his followers formed a new race of gods who lived on the top of a cloud-capped mountain called Mount Olympus. From his palace high above the clouds, Zeus kept a stern eye on what went on below. He was not at all pleased when he saw that the Titans were befriending some new arrivals on Earth, poor weak creatures known as human beings. Where these humans came from no one could say for sure. Some said that Mother Earth made them out of rocks and soil. Others said that a Titan called Prometheus modelled them from potter's clay. Prometheus was clever and good at making things. He helped human beings a lot when they were new to the world and didn't know how to manage. One day Mother Earth gave him an enormous basket of gifts and told him to share them out among all the creatures of the world. 'I have made them too hastily,' she said, 'and not finished them off properly.'

Now Prometheus had a brother called Epimetheus who was as foolish as Prometheus was wise. When Epimetheus saw the basket he begged to be allowed to do the sharing.

'No you can't,' said Prometheus. 'You'll make a mess of it.'

But Epimetheus pleaded so much that in the end Prometheus said he could share out just the very littlest things. So Epimetheus gave a shell to the crab, fangs to the snake, long legs to the hare and so on. Then he handed out swift wings to the eagle and ferocity to the lion, and each creature was so pleased that Epimethius could not bring himself to stop. When Prometheus returned, the basket was empty.

'You didn't think I'd manage,' said Epimetheus triumphantly, 'but I've done a perfect job. There was just enough to go round.'

'What did you give the humans?' asked Prometheus sharply.

Epimetheus had to confess that he had forgotten all about them. Prometheus was furious because he thought they needed help more than anyone. Then he thought of the perfect gift for them if he could only get hold of it. He would bring them fire from heaven.

Now Zeus was suspicious of these humans because he suspected them of plotting with the Titans to overthrow him. To keep them helpless he had hidden fire on Mount Olympus so that they should not have it. Prometheus climbed Olympus secretly and stole a glowing ember from the hearth of the fire-god. He smuggled it out in the hollow of a fennel plant and used it to light a fire on earth. This was the best gift possible, for with fire men

had light and warmth, and could forge iron tools
to build houses and to plough the land. They could
make weapons, too – arrow-tips and sharp-bladed
swords. But Zeus was angry and planned
a revenge. He called all the gods of Mount
Olympus together and said, with a kind
smile on his face, that he was planning to
give men a gift that would bring them more
joy than anything else on earth.

'Men are lonely in the world so I have made a companion for them – Woman.' He showed them the lovely creature he had created. 'I have done my best,' he said. 'If each of you gives her a gift she will be perfect.'

So Aphrodite, goddess of love, gave her beauty; Hermes, the gods' quick-silver messenger, gave her liveliness and cunning; the Graces gave her charm. Each god gave something and she was named Pandora, which means 'all gifts'.

Zeus then told Hermes to lead Pandora down to earth. But just as they were setting off he called her back. 'This is for you,' he said, and gave Pandora a box. 'See you never open it,' he added, smiling into his beard.

Hermes brought Pandora

14

to Prometheus but he was suspicious and refused to have anything to do with her. Soft-hearted Epimetheus said, 'I'll look after her.'

'Don't,' Prometheus told him. 'No good will come of anything from Zeus.'

But Epimetheus didn't listen. He took Pandora home and the two got on well for a time. Then Pandora became restless. 'I can't think why Zeus gave me that box,' she kept saying.

'Neither can I,' Epimedeus would reply without much interest.

'He told me not to look in it.'

'Then we needn't bother about it, need we, Pandora?'

But Pandora could not leave it at that. 'I'll take just a tiny peep,' she thought. She picked up the box and undid the clasp.

Immediately, the lid flew open and a swarm of hideous creatures shot into the air – mischiefs and misfortunes of all kinds, envy and greed and sickness and old age, famine and war, deceit, lies, fear and ignorance – every misery, in fact, that has troubled people's lives from that day to this.

Pandora shrieked as the horrible things rose in a cloud past her face and out into the world. It was too late to close the box. There was only one thing left in it, a tiny being that glowed with a warm light, and this too rose and followed the rest. This being was Hope. Zeus's heart had softened just enough to allow people this one comfort that helps them bear the troubles of this world.

PERSEPHONE

IIIIIIIIIIIIIIIIIIIIIIIIIIII

When the world was new there was no winter, or so the ancient Greeks believed. It was summertime all year long. Every day was sunny and rain showers only lasted long enough to freshen the earth, so that there were always flowers growing in the fields, and ears of corn were always ripe and ready to be harvested. Trees had leaves all the year round and bore fruit and flowers together. So how did it happen that nowadays we also have autumn, winter and spring? This is how the ancient Greeks explained it...

The three most powerful gods met to decide how to share out the fresh new world between them. They argued about it endlessly and couldn't agree, because each wanted the best bits. In the end, they decided to draw lots and let luck decide. Each wrote his name on a disc of clay and the three discs were shaken in a helmet. Then they took turns to draw out a name, without looking.

The first name to be drawn was that of Zeus, so he was given first choice of the world's kingdoms. He chose to become lord of the earth and sky. 'I'll keep the Titans and everyone else in order with my fiery thunderbolts,' he boasted.

The second name to come up was Zeus's blustery, rumbustious brother Poseidon. 'I'll take the kingdom of the seas,' he said. 'I'll have a great time whipping up waves and swamping ships.' That left the third brother, silent, solemn Hades, with no choice. He had to accept the third great kingdom of the world, the Underworld, which people go to when they die.

At first, Hades was happy enough ruling his kingdom underneath the earth. His subjects were quiet and obedient, for they were just the shadows of people from the world above. They could never return to the sunlight but they were happy enough in the underworld, unless they were being punished for being very wicked when they were still alive.

All the same, there was no denying that Hades' kingdom was dim and shadowy in comparison with the world above. After a while, he began to long for a little of life's colour to cheer up his icy palace. He summoned his chariot, drawn by two wild-looking black horses, and rode up into the living world to see what he could find.

As he drove through the sunny countryside he saw a group of girls playing in a meadow. One of them was so beautiful that Hades fell in love with her at once. He turned his chariot round and rode straight to Mount Olympus to ask Zeus who this lovely maiden was.

'Her name is Persephone,' said Zeus. 'She is the daughter of Demeter, the goddess of all growing things, who makes seeds sprout and flowers bloom and fruit swell on the trees.'

'Well, I want Persephone to be my queen,' said Hades. 'You must give her to me.'

'That would never do,' said Zeus, looking horrified. 'Demeter would never forgive me if I sent her daughter to live in your gloomy underworld.'

Hades knew it was no use arguing with Zeus, so he went back to the underworld and sat for several days brooding upon his iron throne. Then suddenly he made up his mind. 'I don't care what Zeus says,' he declared. 'Persephone shall be mine! I'll go and get her myself.' He leapt into his chariot, rode out of the ground and snatched up Persephone as she was picking flowers in a meadow. He galloped away with her and the earth closed over them.

When Demeter learned that her daughter had vanished she wrapped herself in a long dark cloak and went out into the world to find her. She searched for five days and nights without rest, asking every living creature that she met for news of her. Not one of them had seen Persephone. She was returning home weary and heartbroken when she noticed something bright caught in a split in the rocks. It was the ribbon that Persephone had been wearing around her waist. Demeter could not think what this could mean, but the sight of it filled her with dread. She sank down on the ground and wept.

While she was weeping it grew dark, for Helios, the god who drives the sun's chariot across the sky, had finished his day's journey and was returning his golden horses to their stable. He stopped when he saw Demeter. 'Up in the sky I look down on everything that happens in the world,' he told her. 'I saw your daughter snatched away by Hades to be queen of the underworld.'

When Demeter heard this her sorrow changed to the most terrible anger. She vowed that she would let nothing grow on earth till Zeus made Hades give her daughter back. No one could make her change her mind. Seeds rotted in the ground, plants withered and died; there was no grass for the cows to eat and no corn to make bread because the ears were covered in mildew. The people of the world were starving and even dying. They blamed the gods for this – quite rightly – and pestered them with endless prayers to put things right.

Zeus saw that he must sort the problem out. He knew it would be useless to threaten Hades, but perhaps he could be coaxed into giving Persephone back. If anyone could persuade him it would be Hermes, the gods' messenger. His winged sandals carried him nimbly through the air on the gods' errands, and his tongue was just as nimble in sweet-talking them into doing what he wanted. Zeus ordered him to try his charm on Hades.

Hermes flew down the dark and narrow passage that leads to the underworld and bowed before its king, who sat enthroned with pale-faced Persephone by his side. She was no longer smiling but looked thin and chilled, for despite Hades' coaxing she had refused to eat anything since she had arrived.

'Great king,' began Hermes, 'my master sends me to congratulate you. You have proved that you have power not only in this kingdom but in the world above. The gods have noticed the great changes you have brought about there.'

'I expect they have,' said Hades with satisfaction. 'People are dying and then they come to me and swell my kingdom.'

'But if the human race should die out from starvation how will your empire keep on growing? There will be no new souls to swell it. Think of that! Perhaps the solution is to let Persephone go.'

Hades put a hand to his eyes and gave a terrible groan as if his heart was broken. 'You are right,' he said. 'Take her and I will rule alone.'

Joyfully, Hermes led Persephone back to her mother, who flung her arms around her and kissed her. But then she drew back in alarm. She had

felt the chill on her daughter's cheeks, the cold touch of the underworld. 'Did you eat anything in Hades' kingdom?' she asked anxiously.

'No mother,' said Persephone. 'I knew that I must not. But once I was so thirsty that Hades gave me a pomegranate to suck and I accidentally swallowed seven of its seeds.'

Then Demeter knew that Hades had tricked her, for no one who has eaten in the underworld can return to life in the world above. Even Zeus could not alter this law, but he made Hades accept a compromise. For half of each year, Persephone must live with him in the underworld, but for the other half she could return to her mother.

Ever since that day, when her daughter is away Demeter misses her so much that her sorrow makes the earth grow cold, leaves turn brown and fall, and winter comes. But when Persephone returns, Demeter forgets her grief and fills the earth with warmth and life. Then spring comes once again.

EROS AND PSYCHE

There was once a girl called Psyche who was so beautiful that people called her the Queen of Love. Now this was a title that belonged to the goddess Aphrodite. She was angry to hear it applied to a mere mortal, and decided to take a look at the girl. One look was enough. Aphrodite was filled with jealousy and rage, and she vowed to make Psyche suffer.

From that moment, Psyche had admirers but none that wanted to mary her. Her puzzled parents consulted Apollo's oracle at Delphi. 'Leave

28

Psyche on the mountain top,' the oracle replied. 'A bridegroom awaits her there and will carry her away.'

So a wedding procession wound up the mountainside and left Psyche on the summit, alone and shivering in the wind. 'Do not fear,' the wind said. 'Leap from the precipice and I will catch you.'

Its voice seemed to be her friend, so although she was terrified Psyche stepped into the air. She felt herself gently lifted in the arms of the west wind and carried through the air, down, down, until she was laid in soft grass, where she fell asleep.

She awoke in a scented garden in the midst of which was a palace. 'Enter. You are expected,' said a voice. 'Your husband will be here at nightfall. Meanwhile, eat, rest and wait for him.'

Psyche gazed about but could see no one. She wandered through rooms with walls of silver and ceilings set with gems, and came to a dining room where a table was laid with delicious food. When she sat to eat the food served itself to her and the wine jug filled her goblet.

Beyond the dining room was a bedchamber prepared for her. Psyche lay down rather fearfully as it grew dark. In the night her husband came and took her in his arms. 'I have waited so long for you,' he said. 'I was afraid you would not come.' His voice was so kind and gentle that Psyche felt safe and happy. But before it grew light he left her, promising to return the next night.

Psyche spent the day exploring the beautiful house and garden, and at night her husband returned as he had promised. Many days slipped by like this and only one thing troubled Psyche. Her husband always left before it was light enough to see him. At last, she begged to see his face.

'If you saw my face or knew my name we should have to part,' he replied. 'Trust in me and all will be well.'

Psyche loved him and trusted him so she said no more about it. But she did say that she would like to visit her family to reassure them she was alive and happy. So the west wind was summoned to carry her back to her parents, who were overjoyed to see her. She told them that she lived in a palace and had the kindest husband in the world. Her two older sisters felt eaten up with envy of this rich husband and wondrous palace and garden, and when they learned that Psyche had never seen her husband, they saw a way to destroy her happiness.

'He dare not show his face because it is so hideous,' they told her. 'He's a monster. He's putting on that sweet voice to deceive you, and when he's tired of you he'll eat you up.'

The sisters made Psyche so miserable that she was glad when the time came to leave. But when she was home she could not get their words out of her head. 'I'll love him whatever he looks like,' she vowed. 'I just need to know.'

While her husband was asleep she lit an oil lamp and tiptoed with it to their bed. There she saw Aphrodite's son Eros, the god of love himself, the most beautiful being that you could imagine, asleep with his lovely face half-buried in the pillow. Psyche gasped; the lamp trembled in her hand and scalding oil spilled onto Eros's shoulder. He awoke and saw her. 'Psyche!' he cried. 'Why did you not trust me? Love and suspicion cannot live together.' And he spread his wings and was gone.

Psyche sobbed herself to sleep. When she told her

family of the husband she had lost, her sisters were secretly delighted. Each thought to herself, 'Eros may like me better.' Without telling the other, each made her way to the mountain top, called to the wind Psyche had described, and leapt from the precipice. But the West Wind did not answer their call and they were dashed to pieces on the rocks.

When Eros did not return, Psyche set out to look for him. She travelled far and wide asking everyone she met if they knew where Eros was, but though everyone had heard of him no one knew how to find him. At length she came to a temple of Demeter and begged the kindly goddess for advice. 'You must go to Aphrodite and ask her forgiveness,' the goddess replied. 'She is furious that her son should love you but you will never find him without her help.'

So Psyche went trembling to Aphrodite's temple and bowed before her altar. The goddess was delighted to see her rival looking so sad and weary, but took no notice of her questions. 'If you can

work hard I have plenty of jobs for you,' she said.
She took Psyche to a barn full of grain – wheat,
rye, millet and barley all mixed together. 'Sort
this into separate piles, one of each kind,' she
ordered. 'And get it done by nightfall or you will
be punished.'

Psyche set about this hopeless task but after an hour she had not sorted more than a cupful. Then she saw a colony of black ants crossing the barn floor. Each insect picked up a grain in its feelers and placed it in the correct pile. To and fro they went, criss-crossing each other nimbly all day until by evening all the grain was sorted.

Aphrodite was not at all pleased to see the task was done. 'Someone's been helping you – that's cheating!' she cried. She flung Psyche a crust of bread and left her for the night.

The next day, she told Psyche to fetch wool from a flock of golden sheep grazing on the other side of the river. Psyche was about to wade across when she heard the reeds at the water's edge whispering to her. 'Don't cross the river now,' they said. 'The rams in the flock are savage and will tear you to pieces. Wait till the midday sun has made them dozy and then you can gather the wool that clings to the brambles.' Psyche did as they said and brought Aphrodite an armful of golden wool.

This made Aphrodite angrier than ever. She had not expected Psyche to return safely after collecting the wool. 'Go to the Land of the Dead,' she ordered, 'and ask Persephone to put a little of her beauty in this casket for me. I need it to wipe away the worry lines that my son's behaviour has put upon my face.'

Once again, a voice guided Psyche, telling her where to find the entrance to the underworld, how she must have a coin ready to pay the ferryman who rows the dead across to Hades's kingdom, and how she must take some sweet cakes to throw to Cerberus, the three-headed dog who bars the way to all who try to leave. 'But do not look inside the casket,' the voice warned.

Psyche listened to the voice carefully and followed its guidance faithfully. She was treated kindly by Persephone, who filled the casket for her. But when she reached the daylight, a terrible thought struck her. 'By now my misfortunes will have made me so ugly that even if I find Eros he will not know me.'

So she opened the casket to take a tiny scrap of beauty. But the box contained the sleep of death and she fell senseless to the ground.

Eros, who had been guiding and protecting Psyche all this while, sped to Olympus. 'Take pity on us, Zeus,' he intreated. Zeus sent Hermes down to shake Psyche from her sleep and bring her to Mount Olympus, where Zeus offered her ambrosia, the drink of the gods. 'Drink it and be immortal,' he said. So death's sleep lost its power over Psyche and she was united with Eros for ever. And, in the end, even Aphrodite forgave them.

ECHO AND NARCISSUS

The Greek gods lived a happy life on Mount Olympus where they feasted on nectar and ambrosia, talked and laughed, and were free from cares – not like the mortals who were having a much harder time because of all the unpleasant things that Pandora had let loose in the world.

Zeus, the mightiest of the gods, reigned over all the others, and, enthroned beside him, sat his wife Hera, a tall stately lady with a rather stern look about her.

Now the gods were good-looking and skilful and clever, and had magic powers to disguise themselves, and to transform people into animals or plants if they felt like it, but they were by no means perfect. They could be unreasonably angry, they could be deceitful and they could be jealous of each other. This is the story of what happened when Hera grew jealous and lost her temper.

Hera was beautiful and Zeus loved her, but there was no denying that she was hard work. You always had to be on your best behaviour with her. Increasingly, Zeus was beginning to feel that it was more fun lolling around with the wood nymphs on the lower slopes of Mount Olympus. The nymphs were the spirits of the forest trees, and seemingly forever young like them. They were carefree and sweet-natured, and Zeus spent many happy hours with them. Hera was most unhappy about this. She said it made the king of the gods look foolish to be skipping about with wood nymphs. In fact she was jealous, because it seemed that he liked them more than her, and one of them especially. She decided to find out what was going on and put a stop to it.

She was on her way to the glades where the wood nymphs played when a nymph called Echo came running out to meet her. She seemed to be bursting with news. 'Wait till you hear what I've just heard!' she said, and went on to tell a long and rather pointless story of what one nymph had said

and done and what another had replied. Hera let
Echo chatter on for a while because she hoped
to learn what her husband had been doing. But
when she realised that Echo had run out in order
to delay her, and had gone on talking to give Zeus
time to escape and sneak back to Olympus, her
fury was indescribable. 'So Echo loves repeating
what others have said,' she hissed. 'Very well! In
future those shall be her only words. She shall say
nothing else.'

'Nothing else?' asked Echo, trembling at the
goddess's frown. And from that moment she could
no longer say what she wanted. She could
only repeat the last few words she had
heard. Since she couldn't join in the
wood nymph's chatter
any more, she took to
wandering by herself
in the forest.

One day she saw a
young huntsman

striding through the trees. He was so handsome that Echo fell in love with him at once. She longed to get to know him but she could not talk to him. She could only follow him about with pleading looks and stretch out her arms to show how much she cared for him.

Unluckily for poor Echo, this young man, whose name was Narcissus, was used to being admired by everyone. All the wood nymphs were in love with him. But Narcissus thought love a waste of time and made cruel fun of them. He found Echo's silent pursuit of him especially exasperating. 'Leave me alone,' he shouted. 'Do you think I want to see you all the time?'

'I want to see you all the time,' replied Echo, overjoyed to be able to say what she felt. This made Narcissus crosser still.

The wood nymphs decided that Narcissus needed to be taught a lesson. They went to Nemesis, the goddess who brings people the punishment they

deserve, and begged her to make him suffer.
'Let him love hopelessly,' they prayed. 'More even
than we have done.'

Nemesis smiled a cruel smile. 'He loves no one but
himself,' she said, 'so let that be his punishment.'

As Narcissus was wandering through the forest,
he came across a clearing in which the waters of
a clear pool reflected the sky above. It was cool
and peaceful there, the perfect place to rest on a
hot day. Narcissus lay down near the water's edge
and caught sight of his face reflected in the pool.
He was struck by its beauty and was admiring its
sparkling eyes, its perfect nose and sweetly curving
lips when Echo came stealing up behind him. She
wrapped her arms about his neck and kissed his
cheek. 'Get away,' snarled Narcissus, shaking her
off. 'I'm sick to death of you. I don't love you and I
never will. I never want to hear your voice or look
into your face again.'

'Look into your face again,' sobbed Echo.

'You're telling me to look into my face!' mocked
Narcissus, who knew she did not mean to say that
at all. 'Now that makes sense – the only thing I've
heard you say that does.' He gazed at his reflection
in the water, turning his head to left and right
to check that both sides of his face were perfect.
Then he gave a sigh of satisfaction. 'You are as
beautiful as the day is long,' he told the face that
smiled at him from the water.

When Echo realised that his cruel heart would
never love her she fled to a mountain cave and
hid herself from everyone. Grief made her too
ill to eat or sleep, so that in time she became
nothing but living bones. Then Hera took pity
on her and turned her bones to rock, so that she
rested in peace at last among the mountains.
Nothing remained of Echo but her voice, which
will still reply to you if you call to her in caves and
mountain places.

Meanwhile, Narcissus came to the pool each day,
fascinated by the face he saw in the water. Under

the spell of Nemesis he began to truly believe that a being of perfect beauty was looking at him from the pool. He lay by the water's edge all day gazing at it, entranced. He leaned to kiss it, but as his lips touched the water, ripples broke up the reflection and it vanished. 'Come back to me,' he begged, and, as the ripples gradually stilled, the face he longed for reappeared.

Even at night Narcissus could not bear to leave the face he loved. His friends tried to reason with him but they could make no sense of what he said. 'Why does it give me hope, then mock me?' he wailed. 'I know it loves me, for it smiles and comes to meet me when I stoop to it. But at a touch it vanishes.' No one could persuade him to leave the pool. Day after day he lay beside the water until he was wasted away entirely by hopeless love, just as Echo had been.

The nymphs who had loved him were truly sorry to learn that he had died. 'Narcissus, farewell,' they lamented. 'Farewell,' Echo's voice answered from the mountains. But when they came to bear his body away they found no sign of it. In its place by the pool a yellow flower was growing, of a kind they had not seen before. It stood at the water's edge nodding its head to right and left in the wind as though it were gazing into the water. Then the nymphs knew that the gods, in their kindness, were letting Narcissus stay by the pool for ever. They named the flower after him and still, today, we know it by that name, because it is the daffodil.

THE STORY OF ARACHNE

The gods of Mount Olympus were kind enough to human beings when it suited them. For instance, when the Titan Prometheus made the world's first humans out of clay, the gods soon noticed that they had no idea how to look after themselves and stepped in to help. Demeter, the corn goddess, showed them how to grow crops and plant orchards and make vegetable gardens. Hephaestus, the god of fire, taught them to forge metal and become craftsmen. Athene, the wisest of the gods, taught them cooking, spinning and weaving so that they had hot meals and warm clothes. But in return for being so obliging the gods expected people to be grateful. Each god wanted a temple, or better still lots of temples, built in their honour and named after them. They expected people to bring gifts to the temples and to sing songs in their praise. That made them happy, and if they were happy they were kind. But they were very touchy. If people didn't thank them enough, or, worse still, claimed to be their equal in any way, their anger was terrible. One foolish person who forgot this was a young girl called Arachne.

Arachne was quite an ordinary girl, and not
particularly beautiful or clever, but she had
one quality that all her friends envied. She was
amazingly nimble-fingered. No one could spin
thread faster than Arachne or make it so silky and
fine. 'If only we could do work like Arachne's,' her
friends sighed, for in those days, when cloth was
made by hand, all girls had to spend a lot of time
spinning and weaving.

'You need to have the hands for it,' said Arachne,
spreading out her fingers and admiring them.
It was true they were extraordinarily long and
slender. 'That's why I have such a quick light
touch,' she explained with a satisfied air. 'Thick-
fingered people can't compete with me.'

And with the airy thread she spun, Arachne wove
cloth that was a miracle of loveliness – gossamer-
fine fabrics and patterned wall-hangings with
scenes of trees and birds and sun and stars, fit
for the walls of a king's palace. People crowded
round to watch her at work. She was so quick that

the threads seemed to dance into place of their own accord, and as the length of cloth grew on the loom, its leaves and flowers seemed to unfold like living things. 'How wonderful!' her admirers sighed. 'Arachne could charm the birds out of the skies to visit trees like these!'

'You have to judge the colours and effects,' said Arachne. 'I don't think anyone has such an eye for pattern as myself.'

No one dreamed of contradicting her. Everyone praised Arachne. 'You would think that Athene herself had taught her,' said a friend.

'Athene!' laughed Arachne. 'She couldn't teach me anything. A born artist doesn't need a teacher. Athene would look pretty silly if she had to compete with me.'

Among the crowd that gathered in the doorway of Arachne's home to watch her work was a bent old woman wrapped in a cloak. She pushed her way forward now and shook her stick at her. 'You're a bold young lady,' she croaked, 'to boast of being better than the gods. If you'll take the advice of an old woman, you'll beg Athene to forget those foolish words.'

'I wouldn't beg Athene for a bodkin,' retorted Arachne. 'And I don't need advice from an old crone like you. You can keep it for your grandchildren.'

Then the woman grew tall and straight and threw off her old grey cloak. A blaze of light filled the room, for it was the goddess Athene herself. The look that she gave Arachne was terrifying. People shrank back and bowed to the ground. Even Arachne leapt to her feet and seemed about to kneel, but her pride would not let her. 'I may have spoken hastily,' she said, 'and for that I ask your pardon. But let our work prove whether I have said anything untrue.'

'Miserable mortal, do you dare to challenge me!'

exclaimed Athene. 'Then I accept the challenge and we shall see.'

The tall goddess and the young woman set up their looms, one on each side of the room, and began to weave. News of the contest spread fast and wide, and people packed themselves into Arachne's cottage to get a glimpse of the work. Others peered through the windows or waited around outside.

Athene laid aside her helmet and spear, tucked the long folds of her gown into her girdle and set to work. A rainbow design shot with gold and silver unfolded beneath her hands upon the loom. After a while she lay down her boxwood shuttle and gave her work an approving look. Then she turned to see what her rival had been doing.

The people around Arachne's loom were looking worried and rather fearful. When Athena saw what Arachne had woven she knew why. Arachne's tapestry showed stories of the gods, but not in

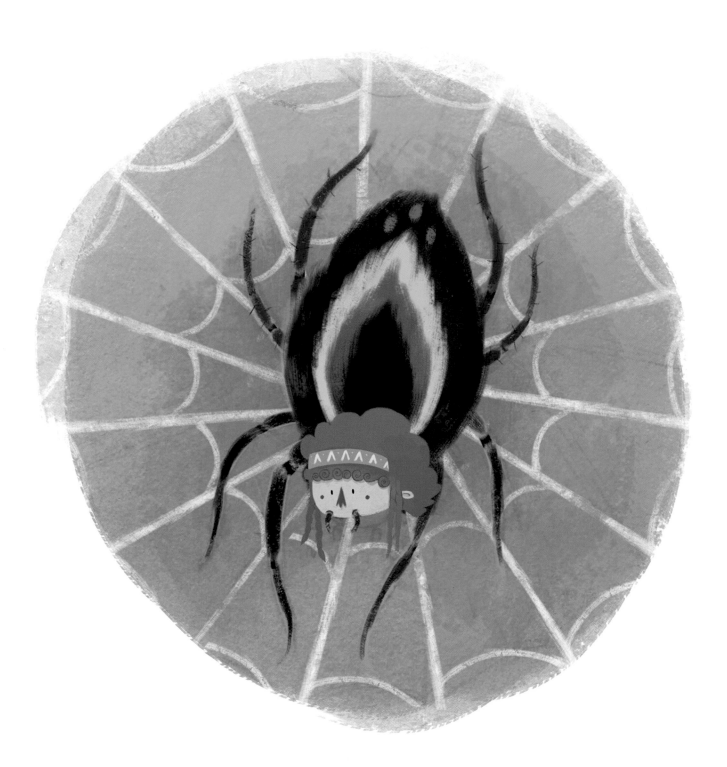

their majestic moments. She had chosen to show the most ridiculous things they did – such as Zeus changing himself into a bull for love and his wife Hera spying on him, green with jealousy. But far more unforgivable than this was the fact that the weaving was perfect. Arachne's tapestry was in every way the equal of Athene's.

The goddess saw this at a glance, and in a fury she ripped Arachne's cloth from top to bottom. 'Arachne must begin her work again,' she hissed, 'and again, and again. Hateful girl, you shall weave forever and no one shall ever praise you or want your work upon their walls.' She struck Arachne on the forehead with her shuttle, and at once the girl began to shrink. Before the horrified gaze of her friends her slim body became round and bloated; she grew smaller and smaller until her arms and legs disappeared, leaving only the fingers she had been so proud of, which now sprouted from her shoulders as quivering black legs.

'Ugh!' shrieked everyone. 'A spider!'

Arachne scuttled away underneath a chest and did not dare to show herself till it was dark. Then she crept out and spun a web across the corner of her loom. And from that day to this Arachne and her descendants have been spinning, and people say 'Drat, there's another cobweb', and brush their work away.

KING MIDAS

When Midas, king of Phrygia, was a baby, wrapped up snugly in his cot and fast asleep, his nurse noticed a line of ants crossing the floor of the royal nursery, climbing the sides of the cot and marching up to the baby's chin. She gave a great squawk and tried to brush the creatures off, but then she saw that each insect was putting a grain of golden wheat in the little prince's mouth. 'This is a sign from the gods,' she thought. 'I must tell his royal parents.' The king and queen consulted the court soothsayers who knew at once the meaning of this sign: the golden

grains meant riches; one day baby Midas would be
the richest king in the world.

The years passed and Midas grew up to inherit
the kingdom. He had plenty of money, in fact
he knew quite a few kings with less gold in their
treasury than he had. But that wasn't the same
as being fabulously rich. Midas wanted chests
spilling over with gold; he wanted golden palaces
inset with jewels; he wanted a mighty army to

make all neighbouring kings bow down to him; he wanted an empire to send him tribute from all the corners of the earth. But there was no sign that any of these were on their way, and Midas was a disappointed man.

Early one morning Midas was walking in his rose garden, thinking how much a scattering of golden statues would improve the flowers, when he saw a pair of of hairy goat's hooves sticking out from under a bush. They belonged to a satyr, one of those rascally creatures, half man, half goat, who were companions of the wine-god Dionysus. This one lay flat on his back with a garland of roses askew on his horns. 'They've been partying last night,' thought Midas, 'and he's blundered in here afterwards and fallen asleep.'

Midas knew that this uninvited visitor, though smelling rather goatish, must be treated with respect. He recognised him as old Silenus, who had been the wine god Dionysus's tutor when Dionysus was a boy. The two of them were still firm friends and spent a lot of rowdy times together. It would be a bad idea to offend Dionysus, so Midas told his gardeners to tip Silenus into a wheelbarrow and take him to the palace. 'Put him in the best guest room and leave him there to sleep.'

By mid-morning Midas was in his throne room, mulling over his disappointed thoughts, when Silenus reappeared, refreshed and beaming. Midas knew his duty as a host and invited him to stay for lunch. Lunching with Midas was usually a dull affair – being so wrapped up in thoughts of gold he found it difficult to say much. With Silenus this wasn't a problem; he never stopped talking. He had a fund of stories to make the gloomiest person smile. Midas was hugely entertained. 'Stay to supper,' he said.

Silenus enjoyed his supper. The wine was fine, the food was good and his bed was comfortable. He was still entertaining Midas with stories a week later when Dionysus, growing anxious about his vanished friend, came looking for him. He was relieved to find him living in comfort in a palace. He thanked Midas warmly. 'In return for your kindness to my servant I would like to make you a gift. Name anything you want.'

Midas gasped. This was his chance at last. He knew exactly what he wanted and unhesitatingly replied, 'I wish that everything I touch shall turn to gold.'

Dionysus looked astonished. 'Think carefully,' he said. 'Is that really what you wish?' Midas assured him that it was. 'Your wish is granted then,' said Dionysus. He put an arm round Silenus's shoulder and off they went.

Midas could hardly believe his luck. His fingers itched to touch something but he hardly dared for fear of disappointment. He was standing by an oak tree at the palace gates. He broke off a twig and instantly it became a twig of gold. He touched the gates. They turned to gold. 'It works!' he cried, and, rushing past his bewildered servants, he touched the palace walls and doors and furniture. He had a palace all of gold! And this was just the beginning. He could pave the streets of his capital with gold and ride in a golden chariot… No other king had wealth like this.

He ordered a banquet to be prepared and summoned his courtiers, who were surprised to see their gloomy king looking so gleeful. They were even more surprised to find that everything around him was made of gold. 'I have great news,' he announced, 'unbelievable news. You serve the richest king on earth. Just look at this – I have the golden touch!' He put his finger on a pitcher of wine and instantly the pitcher turned to gold. 'There will be gold for all of you – as much as you want, and more. Let's drink a toast to riches!'

Midas poured some wine into a goblet which changed to gold as he handed it to his chief minister. Then he raised his own cup, but as the wine touched his lips it turned to liquid gold.

He looked at it, appalled. He was struck by a terrible thought… He took a loaf from a dish and tried to break off a piece; the bread was solid gold. He bit a juicy peach; it was all gold. Every morsel of food and every drop of liquid turned to gold in his mouth. 'I shall starve to death,' he thought. 'No, no, I shall die of thirst long before then. How horrible!'

He fled to his bedchamber. Hungry, thirsty and very frightened, he put his head on his pillow and wept. But what a hard pillow – it was a rock of gold. During the night he dreamt that Dionysus came to him. 'Still unhappy, Midas?' he asked. 'Haven't you enough gold?'

'Help me, lord Dionysus,' Midas begged. 'Forgive

my greed. Make me as poor as my poorest subject, but take this curse away.'

'Foolish Midas,' said the god. 'Haven't you learned yet to be careful what you ask for? But I will be kind and give you what you really wish. Tomorrow morning, if you bathe in the spring where the River Pactolus rises, its waters will wash the golden touch away.'

The next morning Midas stumbled along the river bank in his robes of woven gold. The climb was long and steep and the turf was hard and golden. Midas feared he was at his last gasp. He tore off his stiff, heavy clothes and went on naked. The spring formed a deep pool. Midas plunged in, let the waters close over him and pulled himself out by an overhanging branch. Then he shouted for joy. The branch was green! The golden touch was gone. The turf beneath his feet was green again, he was himself again, a king like any other. But the sands of the River Pactolus are bright to this day with specks of gold.

MELEAGER AND THE BLAZING LOG

One bitter wintry night the servants of king Oeneus of Calydon came running to their master with good news: his wife, Queen Althea, had produced a fine son for him, a thing to make the whole of Calydon rejoice, for everyone knew the king was longing for an heir. The newborn child, named Meleager by his parents, was wrapped up in blankets and sheepskin and put in a cradle next to his mother's bed. The queen looked anxiously at the tiny bundle. 'He mustn't feel cold in the night,' she fretted. 'Put another log on the fire, nurse, to keep it in till morning.' The nurse did as she was

bid and then left the mother bending over from her bed to gaze into her son's face in the firelight.

Althea was sinking back to rest when she thought she saw figures in the room. 'I must be dreaming,' she thought, 'for no one has come through the door.' Yet three women, their faces hidden in grey cloaks, were seated by the fire. Althea recognised them with a chill of fear. These were the three terrible sisters, the Fates, who at the moment of our birth begin to spin the thread of our life, and who will fix the moment of its end by breaking off the thread.

The first sister began the spinning by drawing out raw wool from the bundle on her distaff and twisting it into thread. 'This child shall be brave and handsome,' she said.

'He shall be bold, too bold and very quick to anger,' said the second, winding the new thread onto a bobbin.

'But he shall live no longer,' said the third, 'than that blazing log shall burn upon the hearth.' She drew a pair of scissors from beneath her cloak and sat waiting to cut the thread.

In an instant Althea leapt from her bed and thrust her hand into the flames. She drew out the log, plunged it into a jug of water, wrapped the blackened wood in a cloth and locked it away in a chest. When this was done she saw that daylight was already chasing away the shadows. The Fates had vanished and the baby slumbered peacefully in his crib.

Meleager grew up to be a handsome and brave young man, just as the Fates foretold. He loved all sports and outdoor competitions, racing, wrestling and hunting, and was reckoned to be the best javelin thrower in Greece. The time came when his country badly needed his skills. Its people were suffering under a terrible punishment sent by the goddess Artemis, for something that was really not their fault. King Oeneus had been thoughtless.

He had forgotten to include Artemis in his yearly sacrifices to the Olympian gods. The furious goddess decided to punish the land of Calydon. She sent an enormous boar to devastate the land, a huge brute, larger than a bull. Its tusks were like an elephant's; the crest along its back bristled like a row of spears; its breath scorched roots and branches. It raged up and down the kingdom tearing and trampling everything in its path. It turned forests to cinder, flattened corn and gored cattle and people; villagers threw their belongings into carts and fled to the city.

Meleager announced that he would fight this boar, a suggestion that horrified his father, for it was clear the boar was far too terrible for even the bravest warrior to tackle on his own. The king had a better solution. He sent heralds to all the courts of Greece inviting the bravest fighters in the land to come to Calydon and join Prince Meleager in a glorious boar hunt. Whoever struck the blow that killed the beast should be allowed to keep its hide and tusks as a trophy.

From all over Greece, men eager for glory arrived for the hunt. Theseus came from Athens and Jason from Iolcus, and many others including Meleager's two uncles, the brothers of Althea. Among the arrivals was a tall, fair stranger carrying a bow and ivory quiver. When he took off his travelling hat a mass of tumbling golden curls fell around his shoulders, proving, to everyone's astonishment that this was a woman. Her name was Atalanta, daughter of the king of Arcadia. To Meleager her combination of beauty and hunting prowess was irresistible, and he fell in love with her at once.

King Oeneus entertained the hunters well. They feasted for nine days and nights and Artemis heard their shouts and laughter. She knew they were planing the death of her boar and she laid plans to spoil their hunt. She soured the hunters' tempers and made them quarrelsome. Meleager's uncles grumbled that a hunt was no place for a woman. 'We haven't come here to play women's games,' they said. 'She should go home.' They smirked to see Meleager turn crimson with rage, for it was obvious to everyone that he was smitten with the stranger, while she took no notice of him at all.

Still angry in their hearts the hunters set off on the tenth day, some armed with bows and arrows, others with boar-spears, javelins or axes, all keen to be the one that struck the death blow. The boar was found lurking by a stream amongst some willows. It bounded out, killing two huntsmen and sending others scrambling for safety. It would have done more damage if Atalanta had not let fly an arrow that sank deep into the folds of its neck. It roared with rage and charged again but Meleager flung his javelin into its right flank, and as it whirled about in pain he drove his hunting spear into its heart.

Meleager had killed the boar and won the trophy — its hide and tusks — but when the beast was skinned he presented these to Atalanta. 'You were the first to wound the boar,' he said, 'and if I had not interfered you would have killed it.'

Then everyone began to argue; they said this was against the sporting rules. If the winner wished to give his prize away he had to offer it to the huntsman of the highest rank. In this case it should go to Meleager's elder uncle, brother-in-law to the king. The uncle snatched the hide from Atalanta, and Meleager, furious at the insult to his loved-one, attacked him in a blind rage. His brother joined the fight. Knives were drawn and Meleager killed his uncles.

Althea saw two corpses carried in a sad procession through the city gates. She recognised her brothers

and was told they had been murdered. She raised her hands to heaven. 'Who is their murderer?' she demanded. 'By the gods I swear I shall not rest until I see him dead.'

'It is your son,' they said.

Not pausing to allow herself an instant's thought, Althea ran to the chest, seized the blackened log and threw it on the fire. She watched it burn until it was a heap of ash. Meleager, returning from the hunt, was seized with pains like fire. He fell to the ground and was carried home dead by his hunting companions.

ATALANTA AND THE GOLDEN APPLES

Atalanta, the mysterious huntress who caused such a stir in Calydon, was as strong and fearless as she was beautiful. And this was no wonder, for although she was a princess she had been brought up in the wild. Her father, Prince Iasus of Argos, had wanted nothing to do with her when she was born. For many years he had been longing for a son to be his heir, and when he heard his newborn child was a daughter he told a servant to take it to the hills and leave it there to die.

The servant was a kind-hearted man with children of his own. He wrapped the tiny baby in the folds of his cloak and set off up the hillside and into the forest that lined its slopes. 'Let's leave you in a sheltered spot,' he said, nestling the little bundle in a hollow among some tree roots, 'and may the gods take care of you.'

His prayer was answered, for the huntress-goddess Artemis found the sleeping baby and sent a she-bear to look after it. The bear licked the child, lifted it gently in its mouth and carried it to her cave to join her newborn litter of cubs. It snuggled down among them and sucked its foster mother's milk, just like its bear brothers and sisters.

Some weeks later a party of woodsmen came across the bear suckling her cubs at the mouth of her cave, and saw there was a human child amongst them. 'This will never do,' they thought. 'We must rescue it and give it a proper home.' Too wise to rob the bear directly of her young, they waited until they found the cubs untended and took the baby girl away to be cared for properly.

So Atalanta was brought up among country people who tended their sheep on the hillsides and hunted in the forests. She loved this sort of life and was outdoors in all weathers. The bear's milk had made her so strong and fearless that everyone treated her as a boy. She handled weapons and hunted with the men, who thought of her as an equal. When she grew up they could not fail to notice she was beautiful, but none of them would have dared to speak to her of love. They knew she despised such nonsense. Love never even entered her head.

Her scorn for love was highly pleasing to the goddess Artemis, who had been keeping her eye on Atalanta since the day she found her in the forest.

Artemis detested lovey-dovey behaviour and severely punished any man bold enough to admire her beauty. She expected Atalanta to join her band of nymphs who went on all her hunting expeditions. She gave the girl a warning: 'Never marry, for if you do you will become a captive all your days.'

Atalanta was perfectly content to follow that advice, but events did not let her. She had created such a stir in Calydon that news of the fearless unknown huntress reached the court of Prince Iasus. He sent officials to find out more about this stranger who had appeared out of the wilds. Bit by bit, they pieced together the truth, and father and daughter were reconciled. Iasus was overjoyed, for Atalanta was just the sort of child he had hoped for; no son could have made him prouder. All the same, he felt that in certain matters a daughter should behave as other daughters did. 'Now we must find a fine husband for you,' he said.

Atalanta hated the idea. She would not listen to her father and for a long time he barely spoke to her. This made her sad for she did not wish to lose his love. So she thought of a scheme that would satisfy him while putting off – perhaps for ever – the need to take a husband.

'Father,' she told him, 'I promise to marry the man who can outrun me in a race. Any man may try, but if I defeat him I shall kill him with my bow and arrow.' Her father agreed, for although she ran fast he did not think it would be difficult to outrun the fastest girl. Many young men thought so too but they learned their mistake. Atalanta ran faster than the wind, and although she gave each of her suitors a head start, not one of them reached the winning post ahead of her. Then she made each loser pay the penalty.

Even when it was known that to race against Atalanta meant certain death, there were still many men so in love with her that they were ready to try. A young man of Argos called Hippomenes heard of them racing to their deaths and could not believe that anyone could be so stupid. 'I would not risk my life for a woman,' he declared. But he had to admit that he was curious to see what she looked like, and when the next group of hopeful suitors came to race, Hippomenes was amongst the watching crowd. When he saw Atalanta dart forward he felt as if he were already shot through the heart by her arrow. Any risk seemed worth taking to win such dazzling beauty. Despite his previous wise words, Hippomenes knew that he had to run the race.

He was still sensible enough to know that trusting to his skill as a runner would be useless. He needed help and prayed to the goddess Aphrodite to come to his rescue. As goddess of love she seemed a good choice, for she certainly could not be pleased by Atalanta's attitude to it. Indeed he was right, for Aphrodite listened sympathetically and gave Hippomenes three golden apples. 'Use these as I tell you,' she said, 'and you will win the race.'

When Atalanta saw Hippomenes's eager handsome face at the starting post she felt such a liking for him that she hesitated. 'Do you mean to run or not?' said her father. 'The crowd is waiting.'

Then Atalanta brushed such soft-heartedness aside. She sprang from the starting line and was soon level with Hippomenes, despite his start. As he ran he rolled one of the apples fast along the ground ahead of her. She saw it gleaming and paused to pick it up. In the same moment Hippomenes shot past her, straining every muscle to keep ahead. All the same Atlanta had overtaken him before the halfway mark. Hippomenes rolled the second apple in her path and again, though she could not say why, Atalanta felt she must have it. As she ran aside to get it Hippomenes passed her again. He was in sight of the winning post when she sped by him again, and in desperation he thew the last apple. Despite herself Atalanta stopped. Aphrodite's fruit seemed to beckon and she must have it. As she stretched her hand to the apple she heard the crowd cheering. Hippomenes had won the race and she was his.

So Hippomenes and Atalanta were very happily
married. He knew better than to try to tame her
wild ways and she was grateful to him for that.
All would have been well if Hippomenes had not
been so wrapped up in his new happiness that he
forgot to thank Aphrodite who had brought it all
about. The goddess expected offerings and incense
to be placed on her altar and poems sung in her

praise. When these did not appear she was angry and went to consult Rhea, the mother of the gods, about a suitable punishment. Rhea turned Atalanta and Hippomenes into a pair of lions and harnessed them to her chariot, which ever after they were forced to pull. So Atalanta became a captive for the rest of her days.

GLOSSARY

Apollo
One of the sons of Zeus. He is a god of truth, prophecy, poetry and music, among other things.

Bodkin
A thick, blunt needle with a large eye.

Daffodil
The scientific name for daffodil is Narcissus pseudonarcissus. It is a plant, often yellow in colour, with a trumpet-like flower.

Delphi
The town in Greece that contained the temple of Apollo.

Dionysus
A god of nature, wine and ecstasy in Greek mythology, who had a cult following in ancient Greece.

Gossamer
A light, thin and delicate material.

Laocoon
A priest of the god Apollo. When he offended Apollo, the god sent two sea serpents to crush him and his sons to death.

Mount Olympus
A mountain peak in Greece and the home of the gods in Greek mythology.

Oracle
Someone who made prophecies about the future by communicating with the gods.

Theseus
A heroic man in Greek mythology, who had many adventures involving perilous journeys and dangerous monsters.